A DAY ON THE FARM

BY NANCY FIELDING HULICK

PICTURES BY JOHN P. MILLER

A GOLDEN BOOK • NEW YORK

Western Publishing Company, Inc.
Racine, Wisconsin 53404

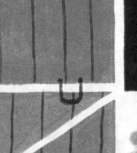

PQRST

Farmer Brown and his family live on a little farm in the country.

Every morning when the sun comes up, Farmer Brown goes out to the barn.

He milks the cows.

He feeds hay to the horses.

He scatters grain to the hungry chickens.
"Cluck, cluck, cluck!" says the old red hen.

The pig likes to have his back scratched with a stick.

"Oink, oink," he grunts. He is very pleased.

When he has finished his chores, Farmer Brown walks back to the farmhouse. Mrs. Brown cooks eggs and bacon and pancakes for breakfast.

"Yum, yum!" say Sally and Sam.
They are just as hungry as the animals on the farm.
Jip and Mittens are hungry, too!

At nine o'clock, the school bus comes by to pick up Sally and Sam.

Honk! Honk! The driver toots the horn.

"Hi!" say all the children in the bus.

Sally and Sam climb in and wave goodbye to Jip as the bus drives down the road.

Farmer Brown goes back to the barn. He starts
up the tractor. It is time to cut and rake the hay.

He drives around the field in the warm sun.
Jip chases a rabbit in the tall grass.

In the farmhouse, Mrs. Brown is baking a chocolate cake. Aunt Alice and Uncle Tom are coming for supper.

They are bringing their two children to play with Sally and Sam.

Mittens wants to lick the bowl.

"Scat!" cries Mrs. Brown. Mittens is not really afraid, but he runs out the door.

It is noon, and time for lunch. Farmer Brown meets the mailman coming up the path. He has a package for the Browns.

What can it be?

Lots of new baby chicks! Farmer Brown carries the box out to the henhouse. When the chicks are bigger, they will run in the barnyard with the other farm animals.

At four o'clock, Sally and Sam come home from school.

They show Mrs. Brown their new books and pencils.

It's fun to play in the yard.
Sally climbs the apple tree, and Sam carves a boat
to sail on the pond.

The children ride their pony around the field.

Aunt Alice and Uncle Tom are here for supper.
Sally and Sam are glad to see their cousins.
Mrs. Brown's chocolate cake is a big success.
Uncle Tom eats three pieces!

The big folks sit and chat on the front porch while the children play hide-and-go-seek. A harvest moon is rising over the fields.

Aunt Alice and Uncle Tom and the children say
goodnight and drive away.

Time for bed! Tomorrow is another busy day.
Goodnight Sally. Goodnight Sam. Goodnight Jip
and Mittens.